Who Took Our Cake?

Heather Hammonds

NELSON

TM

THOMSON LEARNING

Australia · Canada · Mexico · Singapore · Spain · United Kingdom · United States

Here is our cake.

We can eat it

after we play.

3

Oh no!

Where has our cake gone?

We will find out.

Has mum seen our cake?

Our cake is big
and round.

It has icing on top.

We will look on the plate.

We will look on the table.

We will look on the floor.

Look at this!

Can you see

some cake crumbs?

Can you see some icing?

Look at this!

Can you see a paw print?

Now we will look

in the garden.

14

Can you see

who took our cake?

Henry!

He ate our cake.

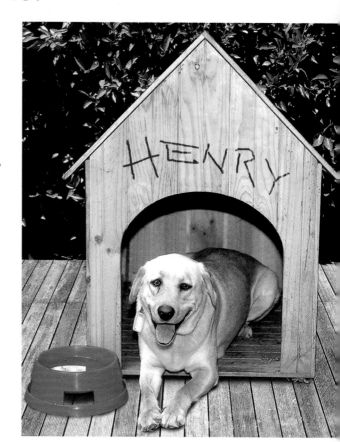